Birds

Tamra Orr

Huntington City Township
Public Library
255 West Park Drive
Huntington, IN 46750
www.huntingtonpub.lib.in.us

PURPLE TOAD
PUBLISHING

P.O. Box 631
Kennett Square, Pennsylvania 19348
www.purpletoadpublishing.com

Printing   1   2   3   4   5   6   7   8   9

WHAT ARE THEY SAYING?

Birds
Cats
Dogs
Guinea Pigs
Horses

Publisher's Congress-in-Publication Data
Orr, Tamra
    What Are They Saying: Birds / Tamra Orr
        p. cm. — (What are they saying?)
Includes bibliographic references and index.
ISBN: 978-1-62469-032-7 (library bound)
1. Birds — Juvenile literature.   I. Title.
    QL676.2 2013
    598 — dc23
                                                                        2013936067

eBook ISBN: 9781624690334

ABOUT THE AUTHOR: Tamra Orr is author of more than 350 books for readers of all ages. She lives in Oregon with her three kids, husband, cat, and dog. All of the birds in Orr's life live in her backyard and wake her every morning with their beautiful songs, chirps, and squawks.

PUBLISHER'S NOTE: The data in this book has been researched in depth, and to the best of our knowledge is factual. Although every measure has been taken to give an accurate account, Purple Toad Publishing makes no warranty of the accuracy of the information and is not liable for damages caused by inaccuracies.

Printed by Lake Book Manufacturing, Chicago, IL

WHAT ARE THEY SAYING?

Birds

A New Home

My head is under my wing and my eyes are closed, but something is different. I listen carefully. I do not hear the sounds of the pet store. Where are the meows of the kittens? Where is the sound of the dogs chasing each other? Where are the other birds' songs or the parrot's silly whistle?

You cannot see my ears. They are covered with feathers. I hear very well though! Where are the sounds that I hear every morning? Where am I? Then, I remember. Yesterday, a pretty little girl came into the pet store. She had a soft voice and a smile. She looked at other birds, and then pointed at me.

It was scary when I left the store. My wings shook, but I sat very still and closed my eyes. Now, they are open again. I am in a new home!

Pet Fact:

Birds are sold by pet stores or from people called breeders who raise birds. Sometimes people adopt birds from bird rescues or animal shelters. Adopting any pet bird, especially a parrot, is a big responsibility.

A New Name

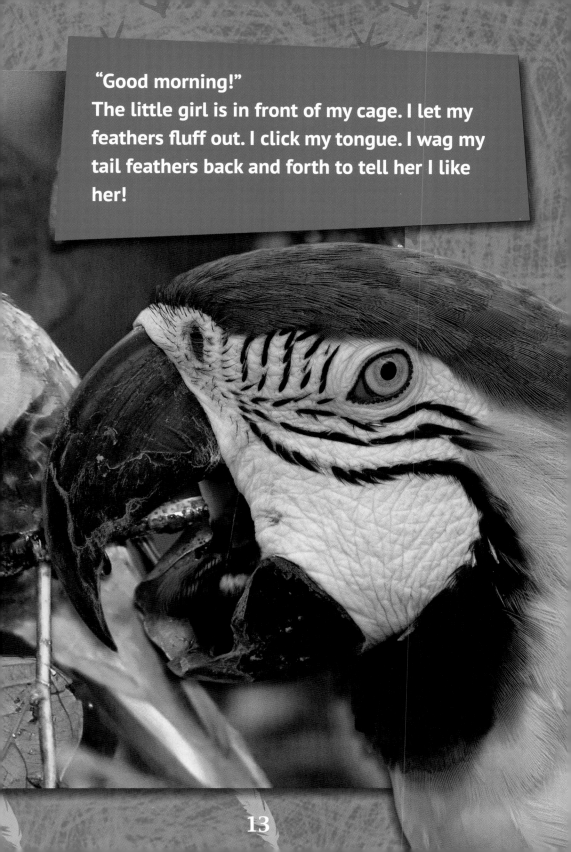

"Good morning!"
The little girl is in front of my cage. I let my feathers fluff out. I click my tongue. I wag my tail feathers back and forth to tell her I like her!

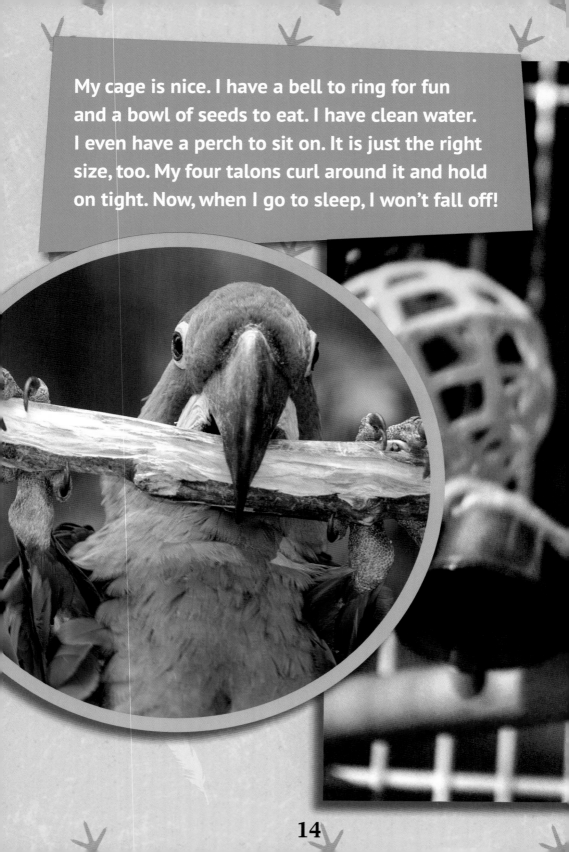

My cage is nice. I have a bell to ring for fun and a bowl of seeds to eat. I have clean water. I even have a perch to sit on. It is just the right size, too. My four talons curl around it and hold on tight. Now, when I go to sleep, I won't fall off!

How wonderful! I am delighted to have my cage so close to a window. Looking through the glass, I can't believe my luck. My girl lives on a farm! I can see some wild birds, and even some farm animals like geese just outside.

How can you tell when a bird does not want to be touched? It will tell you. Watch carefully. Its *pupils,* or dark circles in its eyes, *dilate,* or get bigger. It flips its wings quickly. It can even growl! Stay away or you might be bitten!

A New Song

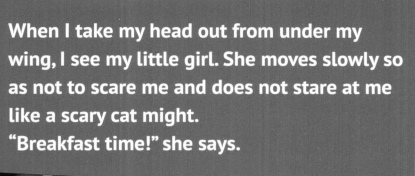

When I take my head out from under my wing, I see my little girl. She moves slowly so as not to scare me and does not stare at me like a scary cat might.

"Breakfast time!" she says.

After breakfast, I take a bath! It is so much fun! Then I preen my feathers to make them smooth. I use my beak to do this. I start at one end of a feather and go all the way to its other end. It feels good!

I feel so happy. I start to sing! I am an excellent singer and very proud. My loud song lets any other birds within earshot know this is my home. I claim it!

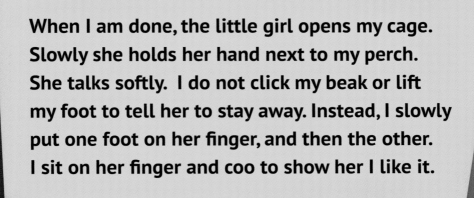

When I am done, the little girl opens my cage. Slowly she holds her hand next to my perch. She talks softly. I do not click my beak or lift my foot to tell her to stay away. Instead, I slowly put one foot on her finger, and then the other. I sit on her finger and coo to show her I like it.

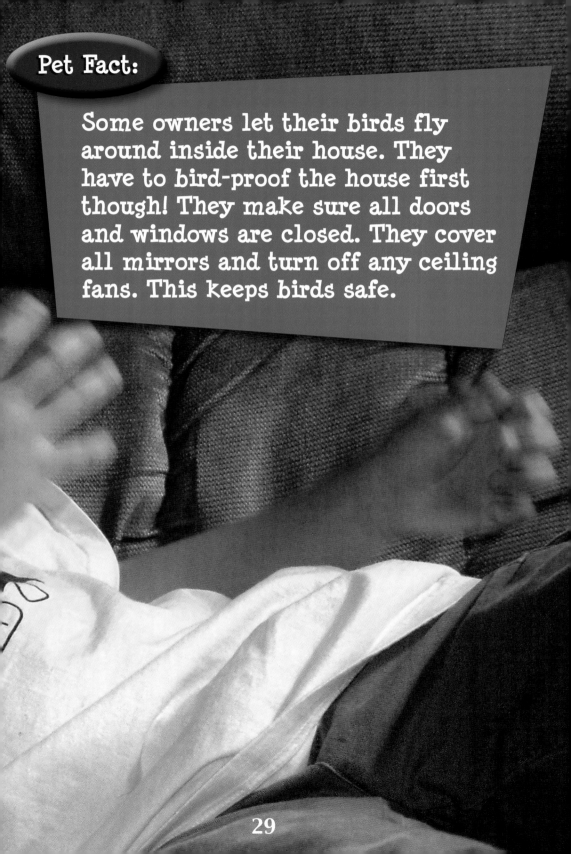

Some owners let their birds fly around inside their house. They have to bird-proof the house first though! They make sure all doors and windows are closed. They cover all mirrors and turn off any ceiling fans. This keeps birds safe.

I have a happy home, and even better ... I am loved.

Books

Bodden, Valerie. *Birds*. Mankato, MN: The Creative Company, 2009.

Bozzo, Linda. *My First Bird*. Berkeley Heights, NJ: Enslow Elementary, 2007.

Goodbody, Slim. *Slim Goodbody's Inside Guide to Birds*. New York: Gareth Stevens, 2008.

Haney, Johannah. *Great Pets: Small Birds*. Tarrytown, NY: Marshall Cavendish, 2010.

Rawson, Katherine. *If You Were a Parrot*. Mount Pleasant, SC: Sylvan Dell Publishing, 2010.

Works Consulted

Jordan, Theresa. "Understanding Your Bird's Body Language." *Winged Wisdom Pet Bird EZine*. September 1997. www.birdsnways.com/wisdom/ww15eii.htm

Mancini, Julie Rach. *Why Does My Bird Do That?* Hoboken, NJ: Wiley Publishing, 2007.

Moustaki, Nikki. "Reading Your Parrot's Body Language." Dummies.com. http://www.dummies.com/how-to/content/reading-your-parrots-body-language.html

Soucek, Gary. *Parakeets: A Complete Pet Owner's Manual*. Hauppage, NY: Barron's Educational Series, 2012.

Unknown. "Understanding Your Bird's Body Language." FunTime Birdy Parrot Lovers Blog. August 18, 2011. http://funtimebirdy.wordpress.com/2011/08/18/understanding-your-bird%E2%80%99s-body-language/

On the Internet

Bird Pet Care
http://petcareeducation.com/bird

Healthy Pet.com Kids Klub—Caring for Your Bird
http://www.healthypet.com/KidsKlub/CareSheetArticle.aspx?title=Caring_for_Your_Bird

HelloKids.com—Choosing and Caring for a Bird
http://www.hellokids.com/c_20671/reading-online/reports/animal-reports-for-kids/pet-reports-for-kids/choosing-and-caring-for-a-bird

Kids: This is How to Take Care of Your Canary
http://voices.yahoo.com/kids-take-care-canary-7147924.html?cat=25

Taking Care of Your Bird—Basic Bird Care Tips for Kids
http://voices.yahoo.com/taking-care-bird-basic-bird-care-tips-for-7188428.html?cat=53

GLOSSARY

bird rescues—Centers where injured birds are taken until they are well enough to either become family pets or return to the wild.

breeders—People who specialize in raising one type of bird to sell.

dilate—To grow wider or larger.

parakeet—A small kind of parrot.

perch—A place for birds to sit and rest.

pupil—The dark center of the eye that controls how much light comes in.

INDEX